This
Treasure Cove Story
belongs to

I AM SIMBA

A CENTUM BOOK 978-1-913265-94-6
Published in Great Britain by Centum Books Ltd.
This edition published 2020.

1 3 5 7 9 10 8 6 4 2

Centum Books Ltd, 20 Devon Square, Newton Abbot,
Devon, TQ12 2HR, UK.

www.centumbooksltd.co.uk | books@centumbooksltd.co.uk
CENTUM BOOKS Limited Reg. No. 07641486.

A CIP catalogue record for this book is available
from the British Library.

Printed in China.

DISNEP
THE
LION KING

I AM SIMBA

By John Sazaklis
Illustrated by Alan Batson

I am **SIMBA**.

I am a lion cub.

I live on **Pride Rock**
with my parents,
King Mufasa
and **Queen Sarabi.**

When I grow up, I'll
be in charge. I can't wait
to be **king**!

I don't always follow my father's rules.

Zazu the hornbill tries to keep me out of trouble.

Trouble is one way to describe my uncle Scar.

He is mean and hangs out with the hyenas – they are the sworn enemies of Pride Rock!

I am brave.

I like to go on

ADVENTURES

with my best friend, Nala.

We sneak into the elephant graveyard.

Yikes! Hyenas!

I let out a

ROAR

to scare the hyenas, but they just laugh at me.

HA HA HA HAAA

Scar tells me I must go away, so I run
deep into the jungle.

There I meet **Timon** the meerkat and
Pumbaa the warthog.

YUCK!

I am so hungry,
I could eat a whole zebra!
Timon and Pumbaa offer
me bugs instead.

My new best friends teach me a wonderful phrase: **'HAKUNA MATATA.'** It means 'No worries.'

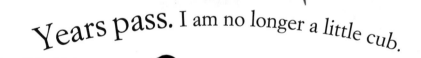

Years pass. I am no longer a little cub.

It was fun getting to play all day,
but I missed my old home.

While I was away, Nala grew up, too.
I am happy to see her again.

I learn that Pride Rock is
in trouble. Scar and the
hyenas are in charge!

It is my duty to make things right.
I ask Timon and Pumbaa to help.

We are best friends *fur*-ever!

When I get to Pride Rock,
I let out a ferocious

ROAR.

This time, the hyenas do
not laugh. They are **scared**!
Scar is scared, too.
It is *his* turn to go away.

Now I am the **LION KING** and Nala is the queen.

We welcome our baby cub
into the
Circle of Life.

I am **SIMBA**,

and I am proud of my pride.

Treasure Cove Stories

Please contact Centum Books
to receive the full list of titles in
the *Treasure Cove Stories* series.
books@centumbooksltd.co.uk

Classic favourites

1 Three Little Pigs
2 Snow White and
the Seven Dwarfs
3 The Fox and the Hound
- Hide-and-Seek
4 Dumbo
5 Cinderella
6 Cinderella's Friends
7 Alice in Wonderland
8 Mad Hatter's Tea Party
from Alice in Wonderland
9 Mickey Mouse and
his Spaceship
10 Peter Pan
11 Pinocchio
12 Mickey and the Beanstalk
13 Sleeping Beauty
and the Good Fairies
14 The Lucky Puppy
15 Chicken Little
16 The Incredibles
17 Coco
18 Winnie the Pooh and Tigger
19 The Sword in the Stone
20 Mary Poppins
21 The Jungle Book
22 The Aristocats
23 Lady and the Tramp
24 Bambi
25 Bambi - Friends of the Forest

Recently published

50 Frozen
51 Cinderella is my Babysitter
52 Beauty and the Beast
- I am the Beast
53 Blaze and the Monster Machines
- Mighty Monster Machines
54 Blaze and the Monster Machines
- Dino Parade!
55 Teenage Mutant Ninja Turtles
- Follow the Ninja!

56 I am a Princess
57 The Big Book of Paw Patrol
58 Paw Patrol
- Adventures with Grandpa!
59 Paw Patrol - Pirate Pups!
60 Trolls
61 Trolls Holiday
62 The Secret Life of Pets
63 Zootropolis
64 Ariel is my Babysitter
65 Tiana is my Babysitter
66 Belle is my Babysitter
67 Paw Patrol
- Itty-Bitty Kitty Rescue
68 Moana
69 Nella the Princess Knight
- My Heart is Bright!
70 Guardians of the Galaxy
71 Captain America
- High-Stakes Heist!
72 Ant-Man
73 The Mighty Avengers
74 The Mighty Avengers
- Lights Out!
75 The Incredible Hulk
76 Shimmer & Shine
- Wish Upon a Sleepover
77 Shimmer & Shine - Backyard Ballet
78 Paw Patrol - All-Star Pups!
79 Teenage Mutant Ninja Turtles
- Really Spaced Out!
80 I am Ariel
81 Madagascar
82 Jasmine is my Babysitter
83 How to Train your Dragon
84 Shrek
85 Puss in Boots
86 Kung Fu Panda
87 Beauty and the Beast - I am Belle
88 The Lion Guard
- The Imaginary Okapi
89 Thor - Thunder Strike!
90 Guardians of the Galaxy
- Rocket to the Rescue!
91 Nella the Princess Knight
- Nella and the Dragon
92 Shimmer & Shine
- Treasure Twins!

93 Olaf's Frozen Adventure
94 Black Panther
95 Trolls
- Branch's Bunker Birthday
96 Trolls - Poppy's Party
97 The Ugly Duckling
98 Cars - Look Out for Mater!
99 101 Dalmatians
100 The Sorcerer's Apprentice
101 Tangled
102 Avengers
- The Threat of Thanos
103 Puppy Dog Pals
- Don't Rain on my Pug-Rade
104 Jurassic Park
105 The Mighty Thor
106 Doctor Strange

Latest publications

107 Captain Marvel
108 The Invincible Iron Man
109 Black Panther
- Warriors of Wakanda
110 The Big Freeze
111 Ratatouille
112 Aladdin
113 Aladdin - I am the Genie
114 Seven Dwarfs Find a House
115 Toy Story
116 Toy Story 4
117 Paw Patrol - Jurassic Bark!
118 Paw Patrol
- Mighty Pup Power!
119 Shimmer & Shine
- Pet Talent Show!
120 SpongeBob SquarePants
- Krabby Patty Caper
121 The Lion King - I am Simba
122 Winnie the Pooh
- The Honey Tree
123 Frozen II
124 Baby Shark and the
Colours of the Ocean
125 Baby Shark and
the Police Sharks!
126 Trolls World Tour

•Book list may be subject to change.